ABOUT THE AUTHOR

M. A. Anderson has always loved things that go 'bump in the night', and that's why she writes dark fantasy.

Having a love of books from an early age led to an imaginative mind, which produced a love of creating stories to amuse herself. From the age of eight she wrote short stories and song lyrics and progressed to playwriting in her teens.

She is an Australian author who writes Urban fantasy, Paranormal and Contemporary Romance. All of her current books are available on amazon.com, smashwords and other online retailers.

You can find out more about M. A. and her books on her website: www.m-anderson.com.au or join her on popular social media sites.

DARK LEGACY SERIES
Reece: Prequel
Dark Legacy
Once Bitten
Soul Chaser

PARANORMAL ROMANCE
SERIES
Wolf Blood
Wolf Curse
Wolf Lover (2019)

OTHER BOOKS
WRITTEN AS MAGGIE ANDERSON
Christmas, Mistletoe and You
A Night of Passion: Clean Romance Edition
A Night of Passion
Love's Twist of Fate
Driving Me Crazy

REECE

Prequel to the Dark Legacy Series

℘℘

M. A. ANDERSON

Bella Luna Books
Australia

Copyright © 2018 M. A. Anderson
Brisbane, Australia

This edition published 2018
Bella Luna Books, Australia

Cover photos from istockphoto.com
Cover design by Maggie Anderson

ISBN 13: 9780992513993
Paperback edition

"Deep into that darkness peering, long I stood there, wondering, fearing..."
~ Edgar Allan Poe

PROLOGUE

Los Angeles, November 2016

My name is Reece Daniels and I used to be a detective with the LAPD. You know, even though I'd been a cop for a lot of years, the things people could do to each other still astounded me. And I didn't like how it made me feel. I'd become jaded working homicide and had been looking for something to make what I did seem worthwhile. The bad guys were getting badder and there didn't seem to be any hope of that changing any time soon. And, more times than not, they got away with it, either because there wasn't enough evidence to convict or on a legal technicality that allowed them to get off scot-free. Criminals had rights. What the hell! I hated apprehending the bad guy just to watch him walk.

It was around that time I met Andre. Andre Delacroix. He was a doctor working in the children's wing at Cedars Sinai Medical Center and I was on a difficult case with nothing to go on: the murder of one of their nurses. I needed answers. And as she'd worked with the doctor I was eager to talk to him.

We became fast friends, and over time best friends. More like brothers, really. I'd grown up an only child, so it was good to have someone to connect with in that way. We had a lot in common on a personal level. He became my sounding board, my confidante, and I thought I was his too. But there was something he was keeping from me, a huge secret, and I would never have believed it if I hadn't seen it with my own eyes. I was the kind of man who trusted my gut and believed that if I could see it, touch it, taste it, smell it and hear it then it was real. Did I have a lot to learn?

Ten years went by before Andre opened my eyes to the things out there that I had no idea about. Sometimes I wonder what took him so long and then I remember his secret and why he couldn't tell me. But before then I was flying blind. I was chasing perpetrators I would never catch. Today I'm taking down the bad guys one at a time. But they're not your ordinary, everyday criminals, there's far more to it than that. So let's go back to where it all began...

CHAPTER ONE

Los Angeles, July 2004

I was on my way to another crime scene, the flashing blue light suctioned to the hood of my 1966 midnight blue Mustang convertible screaming shrilly as I hurtled along the one ten freeway heading south. I'd been investigating another case when the call came through. Dave Colson, my partner, was already at the location and had contacted me to tell me where to meet him. The body had been discovered in an alley downtown by a homeless guy rummaging through the dumpster for food scraps.

I screeched the car to a halt outside the entrance to the alleyway, flung the door open and climbed out of the vehicle, slapping a police parking permit on the windshield before threading my way through journalists, uniforms, and curious onlookers, and heading down to the scene. "What have we got, Dave?"

Dave spun on his heel. "Hey, Reece, didn't expect

you to get here so fast. What'd you do? Fly?" He gave me one of his cheesy grins.

"Pretty much. So what's the situation?" I folded my arms, my body tense, my gut tight.

"Female. Early to mid-twenties. Caucasian."

My eyes moved to the coroner's guys disinterring the body from the large, blue metal receptacle standing beside the backdoor of a burger place reeking of burnt cooking oil and fried onions. "What else?" My gaze returned to my partner.

Dave's Adam's apple bobbed above the neckline of his T-shirt. "Her throat's been ripped out."

"What?!" I pushed past him and stalked across the alley to the dumpster. "Hey, Jim, what can you tell me about the victim and the injuries sustained?"

He turned around. "Hi, Reece. I'd say she's been dead around twelve hours, give or take. I'll be able to calculate a more precise time once I examine her. And…"

"What about her throat being torn out?" I stood with my hands on my hips.

Jim walked over to the gurney and lifted the flap on the black body bag.

I followed. "Jesus!" My stomach rolled and bile rushed up my throat. I raised my hand to my mouth and coughed.

"Yeah, and to answer your question, I can't explain that yet. Like I said, I'll let you know as soon as I do a thorough exam back at the lab." Jim frowned as the guys loaded the body into the van. "Off the record." He turned his gaze back to me. "It looks like something an animal, like a bear or wolf or something big would do. If a person did that…" he said, shaking his head, "hell, then I don't know."

I rested my hand on his shoulder. "Are you okay?"

He gave a heavy sigh. "Not really, no. I think I need a new line of work. Seeing young people killed, especially like that, is getting too much."

"Hang in there. You're the only one I trust to do a thorough job. We need to catch this sonofabitch soon."

Jim nodded. "Yeah, you do." He removed the cream colored latex gloves from his hand, balled them up and dropped them into his kit then lifted it off the ground. "I'll be in touch as soon as I have something."

"Thanks, Jim. Appreciate it."

Dave gave the coroner a nod as he passed then joined me in front of the dumpster. "What do you think? Gruesome, huh?"

"Yeah, you could definitely say that. I have no idea at this point. Let's find out who she was, who she knew and where she'd been prior to her death."

"Got it." Dave headed back along the alley toward the street.

"And, Dave…"

He stopped and glanced over his shoulder at me. "Yeah?"

"ASAP. We need to get some kind of lead on whoever did this and find them before they do it again."

"You bet."

The white coroner's van eased past me and my gaze

locked onto it. *Who would rip out a young woman's throat? What had she done to justify someone doing something like that to her? Nothing!*

CHAPTER TWO

My boss was in his office on the phone when I knocked and he waved me in. This new investigation had him on edge. His ulcer had flared up and he was chewing antacid tablets like candy. Too many young people were dying in LA and he wanted to put a stop to it. He finished the heated call, slammed the receiver down and heaved a huge sigh. "That was the DA. He's already on my back about this new murder. Have you got anything yet?"

I slumped into the chair in front of his desk, crossed one leg over the other and clasped my hands across my stomach. "Nothing yet. I'm waiting on Jim's findings. Hopefully we'll have a name by then too."

"There are too many young people being picked off in one way or another, either by drugs, accidents or murder. What's wrong with this city?"

"People are not as compassionate as they used to be, Chief."

His eyes locked onto me. "Well it's a hell of a way to live, isn't it?"

I shrugged. "Unfortunately, yes, but that's how it is."

Dave appeared at the open doorway. "Hey, Chief. We just got a name on the victim. Chelsea Murdoch, twenty two years of age, lives... lived here in LA and worked at Cedars Sinai Medical Center."

"Have you got an address for the parents?" I was on my feet.

Dave sifted through the papers in his hand. "Uh, yeah, why?"

"We'll go together."

"Keep me up to speed, Reece," the chief said. "And be gentle with the family."

I frowned over my shoulder at him. "I know how to handle it."

He gave me a skeptical smile and waved us out of his office.

"I handle this kind of thing ok, right?" I gave Dave a disgruntled frown.

Dave didn't answer.

I stopped and grabbed his arm. "Wait. What are you saying?"

"I didn't say anything."

"That's what I mean. Do you think I have no empathy for people at a time like this?"

Dave sighed. "It's not that. It's just... well, you want answers. And rightly so. It's the only way we're gonna solve any case. But when a parent's just found out their child is... you know, maybe it isn't such a good idea to berate them with questions." He shrugged. "Ya know?"

"Berate them?"

"Maybe not berate so much, inundate them."

I sighed and continued toward the workroom door. Good to know what your colleagues think of you. "I'll wait in the car and you can go tell them their daughter's dead."

"Reece?"

I kept walking. I wasn't in the mood.

80 CB

By the time we reached Glendale it was late afternoon. Dave pulled the car into the curb opposite the Murdoch house and turned off the engine. The twenty five minute drive had been relatively quiet because I was still brooding over what he'd said. He wasn't just a work colleague he was also a friend and I couldn't get my mind around the fact that he thought I had no tact. Why hadn't he said something before now?

Dave gave me an uncertain sideward glance and I caught it out of the corner of my eye. "Are you coming in?" he asked.

I ran my eyes over the white, single story home with terracotta tile roof, bay front window and well-kept yard. "I think I'll sit this one out."

"Look, you asked for my opinion and now you're not happy because I gave it." He shrugged.

"I thought you'd say I handled these kinds of situations well. I didn't expect you to tell me I was unfeeling."

Dave huffed out a sigh. "That's not what I said."

"Well you may as well have."

"Ok. Fine." He swung open the door and stepped out of the car. "Sulk if you want. I have a job to do." Dave stalked across the street. He hated having to do this kind of thing on his own.

I watched him knock, show his badge to the mother and step inside. It would be the first time he'd have to be the bearer of bad news alone.

When Dave emerged from the Murdoch home an hour later he looked disturbed. It was always a difficult task telling a mother her child was lying dead in the morgue. When he crossed the street, opened the driver's door and climbed in his face was pale.

"How'd it go?"

"How do you think? The mother almost passed out on me. I had to quiet her down, make her a cup of tea and sit with her. She wouldn't let me call her husband. She said she'd be ok, that he'd be home any minute."

Right at that moment, a pale green Nissan sedan pulled into the drive. Before the driver had a chance to exit the vehicle, the front door of the house flew open and the woman ran to the car sobbing uncontrollably.

CHAPTER THREE

Evan's eyes snapped open and his chest heaved as he tried to suck a large mouthful of air into his lungs, but they wouldn't expand. He opened his mouth wider and dragged a thin wisp down the back of his dry throat and coughed. He lay sprawled on his bed naked, the warm tendrils of early morning breeze wafting in through the open window caressed his heated skin, causing a trail of goosebumps to spread all over his body. His temperature was up. Maybe he was coming down with something. He stared up at the peeling white paint on the ceiling and frowned. This had been the second or third time he'd blacked out. It seemed that whenever there was a full moon he had no recollection of his movements or whereabouts and woke up totally drained of energy.

He'd thought about seeing a doctor but decided against it in case they thought he was crazy and wanted to lock him up. He couldn't stand being confined. That *would* send him around the bend. Evan eased his tall, muscular frame off the single mattress and stood up. He felt like he'd run a marathon. Every muscle ached. He inhaled again and this time he was able to fill his lungs to maximum capacity, holding it for as long as he could to calm his nervous system, then letting it out in a noisy rush. It helped. He felt the tension drain from his body.

Evan gazed around the room. *What time is it?* His eyes moved to the clock on his bedside table. The red digital display glowed 4:04 AM at him. He had to be at work by six so there wasn't any point in trying to go back to sleep. He walked across to the small bathroom, flicked on the light and stepped inside. Gazing at his pallid reflection in the mirror, he ran his hand over his unshaven face and sighed. He didn't look well. Maybe he *was* coming down with something. He could call in sick. Evan ran the idea around his brain for a moment before shrugging it off. What would be the point? He'd be cooped up in his tiny apartment with nothing to do if he stayed home. He hated having nothing to do.

Turning on the shower, he took another look at his grim reflection then stepped under the spray of hot water. As the blood swirled down the drain he wondered who he had killed this time.

CHAPTER FOUR

I got a call from Jim Peters around ten o'clock the next morning. The coroner had done a thorough examination of the young woman's body and had sent several samples to forensics. The results had just come in and he wanted to share them with me. We had a great working relationship, but apart from that I liked him. He was a good guy.

Clearing his throat, Jim said, "There were traces of saliva in the wound..." he hesitated before continuing, "but it doesn't appear to be human or animal."

"What do you mean? It has to be one or the other." I swiveled around in my office chair, jerked out of the seat and walked over to the window.

"I hear what you're saying, but it's something else."

"How is that possible? Someone must've fucked up. The sample had to have been contaminated."

"I had the pathologist run a couple of different samples three times and each time they came back with the exact same result. Not human, not animal."

I sighed into the mouthpiece. "Ok, what then?"

"How the hell should I know? I've never seen anything like it before." Jim's voice was strained and thin.

"Not human, not animal. Then what the hell is it?"

"I don't have an answer for you, Reece. But the substance is saliva it has the same properties just not..."

"Human." I inhaled a deep breath and ran my hand over my stubbled chin. "You need to run a new sample, Jim. We have to find this sonofabitch before he kills someone else."

Jim gave a heavy sigh. "Ok. But I'm telling you, you won't get any human DNA from it." I heard the click on the other end of the line.

I walked over to my desk, dropped the handset onto the base, then turned around and paced. *How can the saliva not be human or animal? It doesn't make sense. The sample had to be compromised somehow. That's the only logical explanation.*

Dave wandered through the workroom and came over. "What's up?"

"That was Jim on the phone. He said there was saliva in the wound…"

"Well that's good news. Now we can run the DNA sample through the database and see if it matches any offenders."

My left eyebrow shot up and I gave him a serious glare. "Yeah, we could, if it was human."

Dave's expression went blank and he blinked at me.

"I don't understand what you're saying. What do you mean?"

"Jim said the saliva's not human or animal."

"But that's not possible." Dave wheeled the chair out from under the empty desk behind him and sat down.

"That's what I told him. I asked him to run a new sample. He said they already ran different samples three times and came up with the same result."

"It has to be one or the other."

"I told him that too. He said they didn't know what it was but it had all the properties of saliva."

Dave folded his arms. "Then how are we supposed to find who did this if we don't have anything to go on?"

I mirrored his movements. "Your guess is as good as mine."

"Someone had to have screwed up. There's no other explanation."

"I agree with you."

None of it made any sense. *How could the sample not be human?* Something unnerving slithered in my gut and I didn't like the feeling. Who were we chasing?

ಐ೦ಅ

Later in the afternoon, I decided to take a drive over to the coroner's office to talk to Jim in person. Maybe by the time I got there he'd have some good news for me. Was that wishful thinking? I turned into the parking lot and pulled into a space a couple of cars away from the front entrance. Jim was out front waiting for me.

"Any word?" I said, extending my hand as I came toward him.

He shook it. "Not yet. Maybe you're right. Maybe the samples were compromised due to the environment inside the dumpster." He shrugged. "That's all I can think of."

"Can I take a look at her?" I pointed to the double glass doors behind him.

Jim's eyebrows shot up. "You want to take a look at her?"

I nodded. "Yeah. I want to get a closer look at the wound."

"Ok." He opened the door and we entered the building.

The lab always reminded me of a hospital operating room: Sterile, stark, the astringent smell of disinfectant and death prodding at my nostrils. It wasn't a place I wanted to be but I didn't have a choice. I needed to know what we were up against.

Jim disappeared into another room and wheeled the covered body out to where I was standing. "You're sure you want to do this?" he asked, giving me a concerned frown.

I nodded. "I'm sure." I swallowed hard as he pulled back the cover. In the brutal attack, Chelsea's head had almost been severed from her body. It had to have been some kind of animal. But, then, who dumped the body and why? I leaned in for a closer look.

Jim snapped on a pair of cream colored latex gloves and stood on the other side of the trolley. "You see here." He pointed to the mangled edges of skin hanging by a thread to the young woman's jaw.

I leaned closer still. "Yeah, what about it?"

"The jugular was the target. Whoever did this chewed their way across her throat to get to the main artery. They wanted blood and lots of it. She would have bled out in minutes."

I grimaced. "Jesus!"

"Yeah."

"What are those?" I pointed to a couple of large holes just below the wound.

"I think they're teeth… well, canine incisor marks. It appears that whoever did this tortured her. Those holes are deep and it looks as though the teeth went in and came out several times." He pointed to the jagged edges. "See here? The wounds have been stretched. That was done before her death."

I stared into his eyes trying to comprehend what this young woman must have gone through before she died. "Horrifying."

Jim nodded. "Yeah. She was completely exsanguinated once they got to the vein."

I watched him cover the body with a pained expression on his face. "What do *you* think did this?" I asked.

"It looks like an animal attack to me. A human couldn't do that much damage with their teeth. But the findings say otherwise. Not human, not animal." He shook his head. "I don't know, Reece. I just don't know."

CHAPTER FIVE

The following morning, Dave and I drove to the medical center to question everyone who had worked with Chelsea Murdoch and knew her socially. We needed to get an idea about the kind of person she was and who she knew. As it turned out, she had worked in several different departments: Outpatients, emergency, maternity, the general wards and pediatrics. After splitting up to cover more ground, Dave headed to the ER while I took the elevator to the pediatric wing.

I'd been told to speak to a Dr. Andre Delacroix so that's who I asked for when I arrived at the reception desk. I had to sit in the waiting area while they located him and it was twenty minutes later when he appeared in the doorway.

"Detective Daniels?" he asked, crossing the room and extending his hand.

I stood up. "Yes." He had a firm but friendly handshake. "I'm here in relation to the murder of a nurse, Chelsea Murdoch. You knew her, didn't you?"

"Only professionally." He took a seat beside me. "I can't believe someone killed her. How terrible."

I pulled the notebook from the top pocket of my jacket, flipped open the black cover and skimmed through several pages of previous notes. "What can you tell me about her?"

"Not much, really. We worked together here in the ward a couple of times. She seemed nice. Always ready and willing to help and she was great with the kids."

"When was the last time you worked together?"

"Two weeks ago. She was rostered to the ER after that."

"Is that standard procedure? Moving people around so much?"

"Yes, nursing staff are rostered to where they're most needed."

"Did you notice anyone talking to her that she seemed uncomfortable with or possibly afraid of?"

He thought for a moment. "Why? Do you think someone here might have done it?"

"I'm sorry, but I can't discuss the case with you."

"I understand."

"Do you know if she had a boyfriend?"

"The topic never came up. Perhaps you should ask her nursing friends. They might know."

"My partner is doing that as we speak. How long have you worked at the hospital?"

"I've been here for a few years now. I did my internship here."

"And you like it?"

"Yes, I do. I love being able to help people. It's a good feeling." He gave me a curious frown and studied me for a moment before speaking again. "Am I a suspect, Detective?"

Everyone was a suspect until we ruled them out but I wasn't about to tell him that. "I'm trying to gain a better understanding of the people who worked with Chelsea, that's all."

His left eyebrow arched. "Ok."

"Can I ask where you were between 9:00 PM and midnight Wednesday evening?"

The doctor shifted in his seat and frowned into my eyes. "So I am a suspect."

"Like I said, we're just covering all our bases and ruling people out." I gave him a thin smile. "Minimizes the suspect list which means less work for me and my team." I don't think he believed me. I had a gut instinct Dr. Andre Delacroix had nothing to do with the young woman's death but there was something about him I couldn't put my finger on. I still couldn't rule him out until I checked his alibi though.

"I was home in bed. Alone. I'd pulled a double shift."

"Can anyone verify that?"

He gave me a concerned frown. "Chief of staff. The staff working with me. You can also check the roster, if you like."

"Look, I'm not singling you out. We ask everyone the same questions so don't be concerned by it."

"I get the feeling you think I know more than I'm telling."

I shot him a questioning stare. "Do you?"

"Chelsea and I worked together a couple of times, as I've said, but that's all. She didn't confide in me about anything and our brief conversations were usually basic stuff."

"Do you drive a car, Dr. Delacroix?"

He shook his head. "Motorcycle. Easy on the gas." He gave me a thin smile. "Is there anything I can do to help you find who did this?"

I handed him my card. "Keep an eye out for anyone who doesn't seem upset by what's happened, especially any men Chelsea may have talked to regularly. It's often someone who knew the victim that perpetrated the crime."

"I will definitely do that. I'd like to be able to do more."

"Keeping an eye out will help." I stood up, so did he. "Thanks for speaking to me. I appreciate it."

"Did I have a choice?" He smiled.

"Not really, no." I smiled. "Thanks again for your time. If you think of anything or see anything give me a call."

He nodded. "I will."

As I headed to the elevator I glanced over my shoulder. The doctor was standing in the corridor watching me. I had a feeling we'd be seeing each other again. Something was on his mind and I think he'll want to tell me sooner rather than later.

Dave and I met in the main lobby after questioning everyone we could, then headed to the hospital's Plaza café to grab a coffee and discuss what we'd discovered. He said a couple of the nurses told him that one of the janitors had been interested in Chelsea but she wasn't interested in him. They told Dave that she'd spotted someone standing across the street from her apartment one night and it freaked her out. Had the janitor been stalking her?

The center's chief of staff, Peter Collins, told me that Jon Crane had worked at Cedars Sinai for just over a year and had an exemplary employee record. He was punctual, performed his job adequately, and maintained a good working relationship with members of staff. As far as he was aware, Jon didn't have any friends at the hospital. He tended to keep to himself.

I figured he was the perfect candidate for the crime: a loner with no friends, who was quiet and subservient. I needed to talk to this guy... and fast. After the glowing recommendation, it turned out Jon hadn't shown up for work today. My gut was screaming he was our killer.

CHAPTER SIX

Evan saw the cops heading toward the front entrance and took a step backwards into the alcove behind him. *Why are they at the hospital? Do they know what I've done?* He didn't even know. He'd seen the news about Chelsea. Had she been his latest victim? Why couldn't he remember? Tears stung the backs of his eyes. How many others had there been? Two, three? He'd blacked out more than once over the past couple of months and woken up covered in someone else's blood. What was wrong with him?

He remained out of sight for a few more minutes then headed to his locker. He'd tell his supervisor he was sick and get the hell out of here before the police put two and two together and came back to arrest him. Lucky for him they didn't know he'd talked to Chelsea. Evan slipped out of a side entrance and headed to the parking garage. He'd be home in ten minutes. Then what? Maybe he did need to see a shrink. But what if he killed them too? Sooner or later the police would piece it all together and come looking for him. And what about Jon?

ಬಂಲ

We headed to Jon Crane's apartment from the hospital. Dave called the courthouse to request a warrant on route but was told the judge wouldn't issue one without solid evidence to back it up. Him being absent from work wasn't probable cause to gain access to his residence. Shit! If this guy even smelled us coming he'd be gone and we wouldn't find him.

The traffic light turned amber as I approached it so I switched on the siren, whipped through the intersection and stepped on the gas. I couldn't let this monster get away. The fact that he hadn't shown for work was enough incentive to get to his apartment ASAP. He could already be gone. Then what? We wait for another death? A wave of nausea rolled around my gut.

I swung the Mustang around the corner and pulled into the curb about twenty feet from the front of his building. Dave and I were out of the car and at the front steps in seconds. "Head around back and come up the fire escape," I told him. "I'll take the internal stairs. And be careful."

As I entered the lobby a woman carrying a youngster stepped out of the apartment a few feet from the entrance. She ran her eyes over me and kept moving. Good. I didn't want to have to explain why I was here. I took the wooden stairs two at a time and hurried along the hallway to the second last door on the right. When I reached it I knocked without announcing myself. The element of surprise could be the advantage here. No answer. I leaned in to listen. Someone was inside.

I raised my hand to knock again when the door swung open and Dave appeared in the doorway. "What are you doing inside his apartment?" I frowned at him as I stepped over the threshold.

"The window's open and no one's here."

"That doesn't give us unlimited access. Whatever we find would be inadmissible in court." I marched along the short hallway and into the living room. Dave followed.

"Ok, so we heard someone inside who needed assistance so we gained access to make sure."

I gazed over my shoulder. "Like that hasn't been used a million times before." I stood with my hands on my hips, did a complete 360 degree turn and spotted something. "What's that?"

Dave and I walked across the room.

Blood.

Could it be Chelsea's blood? We'd need to get a sample.

"Dave."

"Yeah?"

"Go down to my car and grab a couple of evidence bags from the trunk."

"You keep evidence bags in your trunk?"

"Don't be smartass, just go get them."

While he was gone I took a quick look around.

When Dave came back I asked him to check the

bathroom cabinet for some Q-tips so I could collect a sample. There was a fair amount of blood on the linoleum in the kitchen. Was this where Chelsea had been killed?

After looking around without disturbing anything we were about to leave when someone came up the fire escape. Both Dave and I swung around and drew our weapons. "Stop!" I yelled.

Whoever was out there took off down the steps, the grated metal clanging beneath their fast-paced footsteps.

Dave flew out the front door and headed to the emergency exit at the rear of the building in an attempt to cut the person off before they got away. I followed the intruder down the fire escape stairs. "Stop!" I yelled again. He kept running.

By the time I jumped off the bottom rung of the ladder the guy was nowhere to be seen. I raced along the alley and almost collided with Dave rounding the corner of the apartment block.

"Where'd he go?" he asked, panting.

"I don't know. He was gone before I hit the pavement."

"Dammit!" Dave rested his hands on his knees and leaned forward trying to catch his breath. "Do you... think it... was him?"

"Could've been. Now he knows we're on to him he'll lay low." I gazed up at the open window. "Let's get back up there and have thorough look around. If he killed Chelsea her purse and phone have to be in that apartment."

REECE

We headed to the front of the building, checking the street and the people in it as we went. No sign of the hooded perp.

Once inside Jon Crane's apartment, we checked cupboards, drawers, under the sofa cushions, in the trash. Nothing. We moved to his bedroom. If Chelsea had been in his apartment he made sure to get rid of any evidence. We were about to leave when Dave reminded me that we hadn't checked the closet. Should have been the first place we looked.

As he pulled the door back a body tumbled out.

CHAPTER SEVEN

It turned out Jon Crane had been dead longer than Chelsea so my gut was way off with him being her killer. The way she'd died was still a mystery to all of us. Who tears out someone's throat? From the information gleaned from staff who knew her, she was a nice young woman who had a lot of friends and no enemies. What about the stalker? If it wasn't Jon Crane then who was it?

That evening, I sat on my sofa with the file information spread out across the coffee table going over what we had so far, which was pretty much nothing. The blood in Jon's apartment was his so we were back to square one. Where had Chelsea been killed? Her car was missing from the hospital parking garage and wasn't at her residence, so she didn't go home after her last shift. Where'd she go? Could someone have been waiting at the car and took her from there?

Too many questions and not enough answers ran around my brain. We had to find whoever killed her before they did it again.

My cell phone buzzed and I snatched it off the table and flipped it open. "Detective Daniels speaking."

"Hey, it's me," Dave said, "We've found Chelsea's car. You'll wanna come take a look." I wrote down the location and was on my feet and out the front door in seconds. This could be the break we needed.

ঔৎ

Andre knocked on the carved wooden door and waited. He knew Adrian was home because he'd been holed up in his writer's cave over the past few weeks completing his latest novel. The external overhead light showered him in a warm amber glow and the door opened. "Good to see, Andre. Come in."

"Thanks." He stepped into the downstairs entry hall then followed Adrian upstairs to the living room. The author had purchased Rudolf Valentino's Falcon Lair a couple of years before for its old world charm, land mass and wonderful views. It was the perfect author's retreat.

"What's on your mind?" Adrian motioned for Andre to step into the living room ahead of him then followed him in.

"You heard about the young woman who was found in the dumpster?" Andre took a seat in one of the armchairs opposite the buttoned, burgundy leather sofa.

"Yes, why?"

"I knew her. We worked together a couple of times."

Adrian sat in the armchair next to Andre. "I'm sorry to hear that. Are you all right?"

"Not really. I've been questioned and I think the detective believed me, but…"

"What if he finds out about you?" The older man leaned on the chair arm between them.

"Yes."

"Your identity is well hidden, Andre, I don't think it will be a problem. Because you can walk in the daylight it would be difficult for anyone to prove otherwise."

Andre gave him a serious stare. "I hope you're right."

"There's another reason you came by, isn't there?"

"I think I have an idea of what killed her."

"Werewolf?"

Andre's eyebrows rose. "How'd you know?"

"Her throat being torn out was an indication."

"But it could have been a ravenous vampire."

"That's true, but I don't believe so. Wasn't there a full moon on the night she died? You have someone in mind, don't you?"

It always amazed Andre how Adrian could pick up on what he was thinking. Well, he was a vampire after all.

"There's a guy at the hospital who I've seen watching Chelsea. He has a dark soul and I sensed that he's a relatively new werewolf. He's confused and angry. He loses large chunks of time and doesn't remember what he did during those hours."

"Why didn't you tell the police?"

"Oh, right. Excuse me, Detective Daniels, I have a theory that a guy working here at the hospital is a werewolf and that he's the one who killed Chelsea Murdoch." Andre gave Adrian an incredulous stare. "How well do you think that would go down? He might begin to think I did it."

Adrian gave him a thin smile. "I meant why didn't you tell the detective you'd seen the fellow watching her?"

"Oh. I probably should have." Andre got up off the sofa and paced. "What if he does it again?"

"He's bound to. After all, it's in his nature. He'll have no control over his actions when the next full moon appears."

Andre stopped and spun around. "Then we have to do something to stop him."

"What do you suggest?"

"I don't know." Andre threw his hands up. "But we can't let it happen again."

"Perhaps you should talk to the detective. At least give him the fellow's name so he can be investigated."

Andre pulled the card Reece Daniels had given him out of his wallet and stared at the cell phone number. "I think you're right."

ᏏᎧᏣ

As I turned onto Griffith Park Drive and headed to the old LA Zoo my gut tightened. Was this where Chelsea had been taken and murdered? Such a desolate location to find yourself in during your final moments of life. She must have been terrified. I pulled off to the side and climbed out of my Mustang. Three police cruisers, a forensics van and a flatbed tow truck sat out front. Dave had been waiting for my arrival and came across to meet me.

"Her yellow Volkswagen was hidden in the grounds. Some kids exploring the site found it and called it in."

"Was she killed here?" I needed to know.

Dave glanced over his shoulder at the rundown zoo then looked at me. "I'd say so. There's a lot of blood in and around her car."

"Jesus." I inhaled a deep breath and blew it out. So my suspicions were correct. "Ok, let's go in.

CHAPTER EIGHT

My cell phone rang just as Dave and I reached the crime scene and I stopped to answer it. "Detective Daniels speaking." It was Andre Delacroix. He said he needed to talk to me about something and could we meet. "I'm at a crime scene right now." I glanced at my watch. It was already eight o'clock and I wasn't sure how long the investigation would take. "How about I meet you around nine thirty at the Library Bar on West 6th Street? Does that suit you?" The doctor said he'd be there and I ended the call.

The pale yellow paintwork on the Volkswagen Bug was smeared with bloody hand prints. I hoped one of those prints would yield a name to whoever did this. Dave and I snapped on a pair of surgical gloves, pulled a small flashlight from the pockets of our jackets and circled the vehicle. No footprints other than Chelsea's. So how did the killer do the deed without leaving any physical evidence behind?

Dave moved around to the driver's door and I leaned into the passenger side. Blood everywhere. The spray pattern on the ceiling of the car indicated that Chelsea had been attacked in her vehicle.

One of the forensic guys came over to us. "Hey, Reece, Dave. Pretty bad, huh?"

I stepped back out of the open door and straightened up. "Yeah. What did you find?"

"Animal hair in the car."

Dave and I frowned at him. "Animal hair?" I gave him a questioning stare.

"Yeah. Do you know if the victim had a pet with her?"

"You think she had a dog in the car?" Dave circled the vehicle and stopped beside me.

"Possibly." He held up a plastic evidence bag. "Otherwise I don't know how to explain this."

I snatched it from his hand and shone my flashlight on it, studying the long strands of gray fur inside. "We'll check with the parents. But I wouldn't have thought so seeing as she went missing after leaving the hospital. Anything else?" I handed the bag back.

"We managed to get a set of prints other than the victim's but they're not human."

There's that phrase again.

"How can they not be human?"

"It looks like…" he thought for a moment, "a dog's or wolf's paw print. That's why I asked if the victim had a pet. Although it would've had to have been a pretty big dog."

Dave and I gave each other a concerned look.

"Where'd you find the print?" I asked.

"On the dashboard."

"That makes no sense."

"I know it. But that's where it was."

"And there were no others?"

"Nope."

"Maybe the fur belongs to the paw print." Dave's eyes moved to the interior of the car.

If that were true, what were we dealing with?

෨ೞ

I pulled into a parking spot opposite the bar, turned off the engine and sat for a moment. I'd driven here straight from the crime scene and I was beat. I glanced out of the window and spotted Andre Delacroix waiting on the sidewalk outside the double glass and metal doors. I liked the Library Bar for its bookish décor, good food, and the beer. I sighed, pulled the keys from the ignition and climbed out of the Mustang. I was hoping this wouldn't take long.

As I crossed the street the doctor stepped up to me, hand extended. "Thanks for meeting me on such short notice. I know how busy you are."

"No problem. Let's order a drink, find a seat and then we can discuss whatever it is you want to tell me. Ok? It's been a long day."

"Sure." He nodded and followed me inside.

It was late, but funnily enough the doctor didn't look tired at all. That something I couldn't quite put my finger on prodded the back of mind. There was more to the good doctor than what was on the surface. That much I knew.

We headed inside and pushed through the crowd to the gray marbled counter. I ordered a couple of beers and some of their garlic parmesan fries, then we headed to a buttoned faux, yellow leather sofa and took a seat in the corner next to the over stacked bookshelves. I could tell Andre was uncomfortable in the noisy surroundings so I offered him some fries to help him focus on something else for a moment. He said thanks but he'd already eaten. That was ok. More for me. I hadn't had anything since lunch.

He settled back on the sofa. "Busy place."

"Yeah, the food's good here though. So are the drinks."

"Mm." His eyes roamed the room and the patrons.

"What did you want to tell me, Andre. You don't mind if I call you by your first name, do you? You can call me by mine if you like."

"Not at all… and thanks." He folded his arms. "I… there's a ward attendant that I wanted to tell you about. Evan."

I eyed him curiously. "Does he have a last name?"

Andre cleared his throat. "Uh, yes, Evan Reed."

"What about Evan Reed?" I bit into a fry, the garlic parmesan tang accosting my taste buds. Yum, I loved these fries.

"I noticed him watching Chelsea on more than one occasion."

"Can you elaborate?" I finished another fry. They

were so good! Or I was extra hungry. One or the other.

"It was the way he was watching her. Like an animal watching its prey." He shook his head. "I know how that sounds, but that's how it looked to me."

A shiver ran the length of my spine. After the forensic findings at Chelsea's car location I was starting to think nightmares *were* real. "How so?"

He sighed. "I can't explain it exactly. I just had the feeling he was up to no good."

"Some of the nurses said Chelsea had seen someone outside her apartment. Do you think it could've been him?"

"I wouldn't doubt it. He always seemed to be where she was. It was like he was obsessed with her."

"Why didn't you mention this to me when I spoke to you?"

"To be honest, I don't know why. I should have."

"Was he at work today?"

Andre shrugged. "It was my day off."

"I'm glad you told me. It sounds like he's a definite suspect. I'll get my partner to follow it up and see if he has a criminal record. And we'll get him in for questioning."

"That's good. If it's not him I hope you find whoever did it soon."

"Yeah, me too." I took a swig of beer. I noticed the doctor hadn't touched his. A change of topic might loosen him up a bit. "So what does a doctor do for recreation?"

He gave me a sideward glance and huffed out a

humorless laugh. "I don't have a lot of time for recreation."

"Ok. But what do you do on your days off, like today for instance?

"I catch up on sleep."

"Fair enough." He wasn't making the conversation easy. I gave it some thought for a moment. "Do you like sports?"

"Yeah, baseball. I don't mind watching it on TV when I can."

"Fan of the Dodgers?"

"Isn't everyone who lives here?"

"Yeah, I guess so. We should go some time. Dodger Stadium is awesome. And I know someone who can get us good seats."

"You do?" He gave me a curious frown. "You want to go to a baseball game with me?"

"Why not? Have you ever been to a game?"

"No, I haven't."

I could see him turning it over in his mind. Maybe he thought I wanted to keep tabs on him, which I didn't. I knew he had nothing to do with Chelsea Murdoch's death. "Well, what do you say?" I finished off the last few fries and my beer.

"Sure. Why not?"

"Great. Call and let me know when you're free and I'll organize the tickets."

Andre smiled. "Ok, I will. Thanks. I'm looking forward to seeing a live game."

"Yeah, beats watching it on a screen."

CHAPTER NINE

The next morning, around ten o'clock, Dave and I headed back to Cedars Sinai to interview Evan Reed. No criminal record. It appeared he was clean. Not even a parking ticket, which seemed unusual. Even the most honest person got a parking ticket every once in a while. As we entered the center, chief of staff, Peter Collins met us in the lobby and accompanied us upstairs. He said he'd requested Evan come up to his office at 10.15 and the orderly said he'd be there. Dave sat down on the two seat, black leather sofa by the door and I remained on my feet.

When 10.15 came and went I started pacing, my gut as tight as a piano string. Had the guy done a runner or had he been held up? After a further ten minutes elapsed, Dave and I headed to the staff room, Peter Collins in tow. Evan Reed was nowhere to be found. No one knew where he was and they hadn't seen him leave. We headed for the parking garage, our next stop Evan's apartment. Not that I expected him to be there.

The rundown building reminded me of a seventies motel, which it may have been at some stage. The mustard stucco, olive green paint and compass point design with the street number on it on the front façade was a dead giveaway. We climbed the two flights of stairs to the second floor, walked along the landing to the last apartment and knocked. No answer. Why was I not surprised? I pounded on the door. "Evan Reed this is the LAPD. Open up." I pressed my ear to the door's peeling olive paintwork. No movement inside. Either he was in there and staying low or he'd already taken off.

Dave and I frowned at each other. "Now what?" he asked.

I sighed. "We have to find him." I reached for the door handle and twisted it. The door popped open.

Dave's eyes widened. "Well what do you know?"

I eased the door back and stood at the threshold contemplating whether to enter the apartment or not. Anything we found here would be inadmissible in court and if this was our guy I couldn't take that chance and let him get off on that kind of technicality. "We can't go inside."

"Why the hell not?" Dave motioned to the open doorway. "The door's open. What if he's lying unconscious in there?"

"You know cops use that excuse all the time. Didn't we have this conversation at Jon Crane's apartment? Someday a judge is going to throw that lame excuse right out of court."

"Maybe, but until that day arrives we can use it to

our best advantage." Dave stepped into Evan Reed's apartment. I waited a beat then followed. "Oh, man, the place has been trashed."

I stood with my hands on my hips and ran my eyes over the mess. Where was Evan Reed? Had the killer gotten to him too?

₧₨

The forensic report on Chelsea's car came back later the same day. The findings? A wolf had attacked Chelsea and ripped out her throat. The fur sample and footprint was positive proof. Why hadn't Jim's team picked up on that? And why was a wolf on the prowl in LA? I tossed the report on my desk in disgust and let out a heavy sigh. Nothing made sense and my gut was telling me something was way off. Who moved the body, and why? My back went rigid and I straightened in my chair as the thought jumped into my head. What if the evidence was planted?

Could Evan Reed be that smart? Would he even know how to plant evidence? He worked as an orderly in a hospital for chrissake. He wasn't a forensic expert. And where was he right now? Who had trashed his apartment? I hated unanswered questions.

Dave came over to my desk. "Read the report, huh? Doesn't make a whole lot of sense, does it?"

"No, it doesn't." My eyes moved from the closed manila folder to Dave's face. "But I have a theory. What if someone planted the evidence in the car to make it look like an animal attack?"

Dave ran the idea around his brain before answering.

"You think so? The irony of the car being at the old LA Zoo hasn't eluded me, either."

I stared at him. "You're right. Someone's playing with us. Someone shrewd enough to send us on a wild goose chase looking for the orderly."

"So you don't think Evan Reed is the killer?"

"I didn't say that. But there has to be someone else behind this whole thing. Think about it. A guy who works as a ward attendant and didn't finish high school couldn't come up with planting evidence and hiding a body. If he's our killer he had help."

"Then that makes our lives much more difficult. How are we supposed to find him and whoever helped him if we have no leads?"

"I don't know yet, but we will. That's a promise to Chelsea. We can't let them get away with killing an innocent young woman and possibly doing it again."

"You're right about that."

"Forensics went over the apartment. Let's hope they found something."

Dave folded his arms. "What good will it do? It won't match either crime scene so we're still at square one."

I gave him a serious stare. "For now."

CHAPTER TEN

"We have to find Evan before he turns and attacks another innocent." Andre paced Adrian's living room. Having an uncontrolled, neophyte werewolf on the loose was dangerous. Adrian's assumption that he could only turn on the full moon could be wrong. Some wolves were known to turn at will, depending on how they were created. Andre couldn't risk it.

"There haven't been any more attacks which leads me to believe he can only change on the full moon." Adrian crossed one leg over the other and folded his arms.

Andre turned around. "Maybe he hasn't mastered the change yet. Maybe the moon causes him to turn because he's new but what if he realizes he can do it any time he wants? The streets won't be safe for anyone."

"What do you propose we do, Andre?"

"Find him." Andre walked over to the sofa and sat down opposite Adrian.

"And how do you plan to do that?"

"I haven't worked it out yet. The problem we have is what if Reece finds him before we do and Evan attacks him? He thinks he's chasing a human. He has no idea what's out there."

"Yes, I'm aware of that." Adrian stood up. "The car was at the old LA Zoo. Correct? Now that the police have finished investigating it might be worthwhile taking a look out there."

Andre's eyes widened. "You're right. It would be the perfect hiding place. The police don't need to go back there."

☙ ❦

I stood at the window near my desk and gazed out at the evening traffic and pedestrians below. *Where would Evan hide? That's assuming he hasn't left LA.* I ran the question around my mind for a while. Where would be the perfect location for him to hide without being found? I willed my brain to come up with a logical answer. Nothing. I gave a heavy sigh, walked back to my desk and dropped into my seat. Staring at Evan's face on the computer screen I said, "Where are you?"

Dave came back from the break room with coffee, set one down in front of me then sat down on the spare office chair at the next desk. "Come up with anything?"

I shook my head and took a cautious sip of coffee. "Nope. You?"

"Maybe." He frowned. "I was thinking… what if he went back to the scene of the crime. Now that we've finished out there it would be the perfect place to hide.

No one would know he was there."

That was the logical answer to the question I'd been asking myself. I jumped to my feet, grabbed my jacket from the back of the chair and said, "Come on."

"Where're we going?"

"To check out the old zoo, of course."

Dave's face paled. "You really want to go out there in the dark? Wouldn't it be better to wait until morning? He knows his way around the place, we don't. He could ambush us out there and who'd know."

"If we leave it until tomorrow he could vanish. He might be waiting for whoever is helping him to get him out of the city."

I could see Dave's mental cogs ticking over. "Ok, but we need to organize some back up."

"We should take a look around first. If we're wrong there's no point in pulling uniforms to go out there with us. The boss wouldn't be happy about it, either."

"Yeah. But…"

"No buts, Dave. This is something we have to do alone."

He sighed and his shoulders sagged. "Ok. But don't say I didn't warn you."

ॐॐ

Andre pulled the rental van in between a cluster of trees, turned off the headlights and the engine. "Ok. We need to get in there, find him, deal with him and get out."

"The tranquilizer injection should knock him out long enough to move him back to the cage in my basement. It's werewolf and vampire proof. I had it built for just this kind of occasion and now I'm glad I did."

"Me too, otherwise I had no idea what I was going to do with him, apart from kill him, which may still be our only option."

Adrian's right eyebrow arched. "You don't think we can persuade him to let us help him?"

"I don't think he'll want our help. He has someone helping him."

"Another werewolf?"

"Possibly. If not, then it's someone who knows about them."

The pair stepped out of the vehicle and headed to the entrance.

"This place has a definite creep factor to it. I wish I'd known about it sooner, I would've used it in my latest novel."

"Maybe in the next one?"

"Perhaps. I'll see what I can come up with."

Andre and Adrian's darkly clad forms dissolved into the shadows of the old zoo.

৪৩৩

I pulled into the parking lot, turned off the engine and gave Dave a sideward glance. Maybe he was right. Maybe we should've waited until daylight or brought back up. The place sent a chill up my spine and I could see by the look on Dave's face it did him too. *Oh well, we're here now so we may as well go inside and see if Evan is hiding out here. I hope he is for all our sakes otherwise we've hit a dead end.* His face has been plastered all over the news without any sightings so here seemed the likely place. I pulled the keys from the ignition. "Let's get this over with." I pushed open the door and climbed out. Dave remained in the car. I walked around the trunk, opened the passenger door and said, "Get out."

"I have a bad feeling about this. Maybe we should wait until it's daylight." He stayed in his seat.

"Look, I don't want to be here anymore than you do right now but we have to find this guy before he kills someone else. Agreed?"

Dave nodded and sighed. "Yeah, agreed." He unclipped his seatbelt and stepped out of the Mustang. "Something doesn't feel right, Reece. I don't like this one bit."

That made two of us.

CHAPTER ELEVEN

Andre and Adrian continued along the path past the empty large cat enclosures, heading for the next section of the zoo. Andre now had a sense that Evan was indeed in the park and he followed his instincts, Adrian close beside him. Two vampires and a tranquilizer needle against one werewolf was risky in itself, but they had to capture him before he turned and killed again. There was no other option.

The pair walked through an open, broken set of double wire gates and found themselves in the expansive picnic area. Some of the fencing on the enclosures had been removed and that's where Andre believed Evan was hiding. As they got closer, they could hear a heated argument taking place. Andre and Adrian stepped back against a nearby wall into the shadows and remained out of sight.

"You didn't tell me you were going to kill her. I loved her!" Evan roared at whomever he was raging at.

"I did what was necessary for your survival. She saw

you, Evan. She would've figured out it was you and told someone." The male voice explained without emotion.

"Why did you make me into a monster? I never wanted this!" Evan stepped closer to the figure standing before him. He was at least several inches taller and loomed over the other man.

"You told me you wished you were something special. Now you are."

"I thought I killed Chelsea. Do you know how that made me feel?" He stepped closer still.

The other man took a calculated step backwards. "I understand, Evan, but what's done is done."

At that moment, a voice boomed out of the shadows. "LAPD. Raise your hands where I can see them and stay where you are."

Andre recognized the voice immediately. Reece. He was going to get himself and his partner killed.

The pair remained where they were and didn't raise their hands.

Evan laughed. "You've got to be kidding me. Do you think a bullet's going to do anything to either of us?"

The detective and his partner moved closer, their flashlights shining on both men, weapons drawn. "I think it could do some damage, especially if you try to make a run for it."

The other man turned around to face them, his eyes glowing yellow in the glare of the flashlight. "I'm afraid you'll be the ones suffering the damage, Detective."

In a split second, both Evan and he transformed into massive, snarling werewolves.

Reece and Dave's eyes widened in shock and they each took two slow steps backwards, their eyes never leaving the creatures for a second.

The two monsters leapt into the air towards the pair, the detectives firing directly at them non-stop without any effect. They kept coming.

The creatures knocked the detectives to the ground pinning them beneath their huge clawed hands, fetid saliva dripping from their mouths, canines bared, mouths inching closer and closer to the men's throats.

Andre and Adrian turned into their vampire state, whipped across the lawn, launched themselves into the air and knocked both beasts off the pair pinned to the ground. Andre stuck Evan Reed with the hypodermic tranquilizer and his huge body sagged beneath him. He was unconscious. Adrian sank fangs into the other wolf and snapped its neck.

The two detectives hunkered on the ground their expressions blank.

Andre raced across to the pair and helped them both to their feet. "Are you all right?"

Andre was speaking to me but I couldn't comprehend what he was saying. My mind had turned to mush. I didn't understand what had just occurred. *How could two human beings change into monsters before my eyes? How for chrissake?* My gaze moved from the huge beasts to the doctor. "What just happened? And who's that?" I pointed to the older man standing with the dead creatures. At least I hoped they were dead.

"That's Adrian De Vries. He's a… a friend."

Dave was very still beside me. I think he was in shock. I know I was. My mind couldn't grasp what we had both witnessed.

"Let's go over there and sit down for a minute," Andre said, motioning to the picnic table standing twenty feet away under a cluster of trees.

"Ok." I nodded and gave Dave a sideward glance. His face was a pale shade of white. "You ok?"

He turned his head toward me but I don't think he saw me.

"Dave?" I touched his arm and he recoiled.

"Jesus, Reece, what just happened?" His eyes moved to the creatures lying motionless on the lawn. "What the hell are those things?"

"If you want to take a seat I'll explain it to you."

Dave and I gave Andre an incredulous frown. "You know?" we both said in shocked surprise.

"Yes, I do."

We followed him over to the table, climbed over the bench seat and sat down. Dave was panting and I knew shock was setting in.

"Take deep breaths, Dave. It'll help." I was worried about him. I turned my gaze to Andre. "What are those things? And how are they even possible?"

Andre remained on his feet. "They're… werewolves."

I almost laughed, except I'd seen them change right in front of me. How could I dispute what he was saying? "Werewolves?"

Dave jumped to his feet. "Are you fucking crazy? Werewolves? What the hell are you talking about?" He scrambled over the seat and strutted away from the table.

I turned around and called after him. "Dave? Dave, come back."

He kept moving.

I looked at Andre. "I'd better go after him."

"He'll be all right. Adrian will catch up to him."

"How did you and your friend subdue those huge creatures?"

"There are a lot of things you don't know, Reece. Things you think could only appear in nightmares, but they're real. And they've been on the earth for thousands of years."

"I don't understand. How can things like that be real?"

Andre sat down opposite me. "There's a human world and a supernatural one. Most people never get to see the darker side… but you did tonight."

I let the information circle the processing center of my brain. After a few seconds I said, "Are there more monsters like that out there?"

"Far worse." He rested his arms on the table top.

I shook my head. Logic, that's what I believed in, but how could I after what I'd seen?

"Unfortunately, it's the truth and that's why I can't allow you to remember this conversation or what happened here tonight."

My eyes darted to him. "And how are you going to

prevent that now that we've seen and heard what we have?"

He stared into my eyes and the dark color of his irises transformed into a pale blue. I was transfixed.

"Nothing happened here tonight. You came here with your partner but the zoo was deserted," Andre said, standing up. "Remain here for fifteen minutes and then drive home."

CHAPTER TWELVE

Driving back from the old LA Zoo, I couldn't believe we'd gone out there for nothing. There had been no sign of Evan Reed, or anyone else for that matter. Where had he disappeared to? It was lucky for us that we hadn't utilized a team of uniforms to accompany us or the boss would've been pissed. I gave a heavy sigh and glanced at Dave. "Any theories?"

"Nope. None. I really thought he'd be out there." He folded his arms. "You?"

"Not at the moment. Evan Reed must've done a runner. I don't know how considering his face has been all over the television and newspapers. I was sure your hunch of him hiding out there was on the ball."

"Yeah, me too." Dave gazed out of the window and spotted an open café. "Hey, I'm starved. Can we pull in over there and grab a bite to eat?"

"Sure." I swung the Mustang around and pulled into the curb outside a Chinese takeaway.

Dave opened the door, stepped onto the sidewalk

then leaned in. "You must be hungry, too. Want something?"

"Egg roll?"

"Coming right up."

My cell phone went off and I snatched it from the dash. "Detective Daniels speaking."

"It's Andre Delacroix."

"Hey, how's it going?" It was good to hear from him.

"Good. The reason I'm calling is to arrange that baseball game with you."

"Great. When would you like to go?"

"Is this Saturday too soon?"

"Not at all. I'll organize the tickets and pick you up."

"Ok. Thanks. I'm looking forward to it."

"Yeah, me too. I'll text you the details once I get the tickets. See you Saturday."

"Great. See you then."

∞∞

"Well?" Adrian asked as he stood by the living room window, his hands tucked into the deep pockets of his gray cardigan.

"He doesn't remember anything about tonight. If he did he would've said something or I would've heard the suspicion in his voice."

"Good. Neither will the other detective." Adrian crossed the room. "Now that that's taken care of, what are we going to do about the wolf in my basement?"

"The only thing we can do. Get rid of it."

"Your new friend was lucky tonight. If we hadn't been there he and his partner would be dead or worse."

"I know. He seems to be the kind of detective who takes unnecessary risks."

"Yes, he does. Fortunately for him you'll become a great asset by keeping him alive."

Andre gave him a perceptive stare. "And he won't even know I'm doing it."

୫ଠଓଃ

The egg roll hit the spot. And by the time I dropped Dave off and headed to my apartment I was ready for bed. The trip out to the old LA Zoo hadn't panned out the way either of us would've liked, but what could we do about it? Evan Reed had obviously moved on to somewhere else and the only way we'd find him would be if he killed again. So for now the case was cold. But that wouldn't stop me from keeping my ear to the ground. If another murder happened in another city that resembled Chelsea's I'd be on it.

I parked the Mustang behind the building, headed into the lobby and climbed the stairs. I needed some sleep. When I opened the door and stepped inside I headed straight to the kitchen. I scribbled a note and stuck it by the phone to remind me to call about the tickets for the game Saturday. I was really looking forward to it. Andre seemed like a decent guy who didn't get out much and it would be good for the both of us. I could use a friend like him, for personal and professional reasons.

I flicked off the kitchen light and as I headed to my room, something pricked the back of my memory. What had I forgotten?

Did you love this story?

Let other readers know by posting a
review on Amazon

Visit the author's Amazon page

BONUS PAGES!

READ the first ten chapters of
Book One in the series

DARK LEGACY

CHAPTER ONE

Andre inched his way along the unlit passage toward the subtle, amber glow spilling into the darkness from a solitary doorway that appeared through the gloom. The closer he got the more he sensed the overwhelming vibration of fear bleeding into the frigid atmosphere around him, its intensity so powerful he could taste the bitterness on his tongue. When he reached the doorway he pressed his back against the damp, stone wall and peered around the arch.

The decaying church resembled a yawning cavern. In the center of the darkness a circle of six cloaked figures, their faces hidden beneath hooded cowls, chanted an ancient hypnotic mantra. Their only illumination were six sculptured candelabra, the flame of each black candle emitting a wispy tendril of smoke that spiraled toward the vaulted ceiling and dissipated into an unholy gray aura above them. A male figure, dressed in a similar, hooded black cloak, stood in the center of the intimate circle clutching a sobbing young woman.

Fingers of apprehension gripped Andre's gut and squeezed as he studied the demonic ritual. Something about the picture was wrong—very wrong. He scanned the shadows for a better vantage point and spotted a pile of broken pews stacked on the nearby platform. Crouching on hands and knees, he crawled out of the doorway, up the steps, and slipped into the tangle of wood.

Every member of the circle watched the pair intently, savoring the sensation of mortal fear. They fed off it: addicted to the exhilarating rush.

The circle tightened as each member of the restless group anticipated their moment of gratification. They pushed back the hoods and dropped their cloaks to the floor—it wouldn't be long now.

"Please. I'm begging you ... let me go," the young woman implored through sobs.

"Unfortunately, I cannot do that," her captor replied, unmoved by her plea. "No one leaves here once they become a member of our *family*." A smirk crossed his lips and he gently brushed the warm stream of tears from her cheek. "You know the rules."

"I won't tell anyone you're here," she said, her voice quivering.

The mocking group snickered at the young woman, sticking out their tongues and making licking and biting motions at her. She shrank back against the man holding her and looked up into his emotionless features. "Please," she whispered.

The cloaked figure pulled her to him and elevated them both into the air. She screamed—the high-pitched sound ricocheting off the stone walls—and clung to him, terrified he would let her fall. Without hesitation, he produced a small dagger, thrust it into her throat and twisted the blade. The young woman clutched at the hole, gasping as blood spurted from the gaping wound in rhythm with her dying heartbeat.

The euphoric group cavorted below, smearing the warm, sticky liquid onto their bodies and licking it off each other's skin.

The dark figure shoved her away from him and she plummeted to the concrete below. "Bon appétit," he offered, remaining above them.

Three females scurried, spider-like, across the floor on hands and knees to where the twisted, convulsing young woman lay. Attacking like ravenous animals, the trio ripped bloodied chunks of flesh from the body with their teeth and sucked them dry, while other group members sank fangs into each other's flesh and drank.

The bloodthirsty scene made Andre's insides churn with revulsion, but something compelled him to continue watching. A disquieting rush surged through his body, stirring something deep within him and he swallowed the sensation, trying to suppress it.

Once the frenzied, blood orgy subsided and the sated group dispersed, only the cloaked figure remained. He propelled himself through the air and landed on the platform near Andre's hiding place. "You can show yourself now," he summoned. Silence. "Must I *make* you come out of there?"

Andre knew there was no way out, and from what he had witnessed, he also knew this creature could do exactly what he claimed. He reluctantly pulled himself from the tangle of wood and steel, remaining at a distance. "Who … are you?" he asked, attempting to conceal the uneasy tremor in his voice.

"You should already know the answer to that question, Andre," the dark figure replied, removing his hood.

Andre's body stiffened. "How do you know my name?"

As the shadowed figure moved toward him through the gloom, a milky beam of moonlight filtering through a broken, stained-glass window illuminated his pale features.

Andre stepped backward. "No!" he shouted, the prickling sensation of fear crawling over his skin like a swarm of insects.

The figure moving toward him was his mirror image.

Unsettling laughter echoed around the empty hall, stealing Andre's attention from the creature standing only inches away. He swung his head up and scanned the balcony. No one. Turning back, he discovered he was alone. He didn't hesitate; he leapt from the platform and ran for the doors.

The chilling sound of laughter followed Andre and he peered over his shoulder expecting to see his doppelganger looming up behind him—but only the darkness pursued him. When he reached the doors leading to the street, they burst from their hinges in a spray of splinters and debris. He stopped abruptly and faced his nemesis lunging out of the shadows...

CHAPTER TWO

3:25 a.m. Los Angeles River, Los Feliz Area

In the early morning haze, as Detective Reece Daniels fought his way through the pack of hungry journalists and climbed under the yellow crime scene tape, he knew exactly what to expect. This body made number six in a series of murders committed over a two week period and, as yet, no suspect had been apprehended. He'd given a brief statement, making it perfectly clear that it was an ongoing murder investigation and, at this stage, he was unable to disclose any information. He hoped it would buy him some time.

The crime scene was buzzing. Uniformed cops guarded the perimeter, plain-clothes and uniforms combed the scene for evidence, and black and white squad cars were placed strategically around the scene with strobe lights flashing. Even the Crime Scene Unit was already on the job.

A rookie cop standing point approached him, and Reece flashed his badge as he got closer. The cop nodded and waved him through.

"How did the press get wind of this so damn fast?" Reece asked as he strutted past, irritated by the barrage of questions thrown at him when he arrived.

The cop shrugged. "Beats me, Detective."

Reece strode across to the crime scene. "What've you got for me, Jim?" he asked, reaching a balding, middle-aged man in a gray sweat suit.

"Same as before, I'm afraid," Jim replied, peering over his shoulder as he crouched beside the naked body of a teenaged girl. "Nothing new."

"No wounds on the body?" Reece stood behind his colleague, arms folded across his chest, and an irritated scowl on his unshaven face. He knew the answer even before Jim gave it.

"I'm afraid not. Nothing visible at this stage, anyhow." Jim was in the process of bagging the victim's hands to avoid contaminating possible evidence.

"Then how the hell is a body drained of blood without some kind of weapon being used? Maybe you've overlooked something." Reece was frustrated with the lack of evidence and suspects.

"Hey, I just call it like I see it. You know that. Don't get pissed at me, I'm doing the best I can under the current circumstances." Jim stood up, peeled the purple latex gloves from his hands and dropped them into his kit. "You think I don't want to see you nail this nutcase? Take a look at her, Reece, take a good long look. She's just a kid. Probably the same age as my daughter, Lisa." He walked away from the body, nodding to the guys from the coroner's office who were waiting impatiently nearby. The detective followed.

"I'm sorry," Reece said, giving a heavy sigh. "This case is driving me crazy. The investigation has turned up nothing on this maniac so far, and the DA's office is breathing down my neck. They want an arrest soon. McCracken is head-hunting and I don't want it to be my head he's after."

The two men stood together while the body was bagged, tagged and removed from the scene.

"Are you absolutely sure there are no wounds? What about syringe marks?" Reece was desperate for any information his colleague could offer.

"Nope, none. I've gone over every inch of the victims with a fine tooth comb and there's zilch. Whatever this guy uses … well, it beats the hell out of me."

"There's got to be something we're overlooking." The detective paced. "We've got to find out who this crazy sonofabitch is and fast!"

"Have you considered the possibility it could be one of us?"

Reece stopped pacing and stared at Jim. "What are you saying?"

"I'm *saying* it could be a cop. It's been known to happen before." He paused for a moment and then continued his analysis. "Why no clues? Maybe he knows how the department operates. Could be he's selling the blood to blood banks or hospitals for some extra cash, or maybe he's one of those screwballs who drinks it." His stomach squirmed at the thought.

"Yeah? And maybe the guy's a vampire." The detective gave an unamused chuckle.

"Hey, come on, Reece, this is no laughing matter," Jim chided.

"I'm well aware of that fact. If I didn't know better, I'd probably consider vampires at this stage—*bodies drained of blood*—it's becoming a fricken epidemic." He ran his fingers through his wavy, sandy-colored hair and blew out a long, slow breath.

"I understand how you feel," Jim consoled. "Besides, vampires leave marks remember … fangs." He tapped his right incisor with his index finger, the hint of a smile erasing his serious expression.

Reece studied him for a moment, an eyebrow raised. "Right," he said. The two men stood in silence for some time until Reece's cop instincts kicked in again. "How long you estimate she's been dead?"

"Can't say for sure. Possibly 48 hours. I'll be able to give you a more precise time of death once I get her on the table."

Reece rubbed a hand across the stubble on his chin. "If she's been gone that long why hasn't someone reported her missing?"

"Good question. I'll leave that one with you, you're the detective." He shook Reece's hand. "Well, I'm heading home. I don't like being away from my girls too long, especially with this nutcase on the loose."

Reece watched Jim push his way through the horde of journalists, camera bulbs flashing every which way as his colleague threaded through the pack, heading for his car. Reece remained where he stood, gazing at the shallow water, too many unanswered questions reeling around inside his head. Where was this guy killing his victims? Why teenage girls? It wasn't as if he raped them. He didn't. Why no wounds on the bodies? And what was he doing with the blood? Maybe Jim was right. The guy could be selling it. But what if he wasn't? With the gothic scene so prevalent in LA, could it be used for some kind of ritual? Reece didn't have any answers and he didn't like it.

CHAPTER THREE

…Andre's eyes snapped open and he fought the damp sheet coiled like a python around his body. He sprang from the bed, scanning the room in all directions before realizing what he was searching for was a phantom from another nightmare. He dropped onto his disheveled bed and combed his fingers through his tousled, shoulder-length black hair. He'd been enduring the dreams for six months now.

Why?

Vampires don't dream.

Ever!

When in repose they are … dead.

Vulnerable.

So, why was he having these nightmarish visions? What were they meant to tell him?

Andre lay back against his pillows and stared at the blanket of darkness above him, knowing when he closed his eyes the horror would return. Unable to slip into unconsciousness, he slid the top drawer of his nightstand open, lifted out his MP3 player, pushed the headphones into his ears and pressed PLAY. Bach's composition *'Air'* drifted into his head. The gentle orchestration of the piece finally enticed his eyes to close and he drifted into a restless immortal slumber.

CHAPTER FOUR

Andre slid the patient file onto the counter of the nurse's station and gazed distractedly around the ER. The nurse behind the desk studied him with a frown; she could see that his mind was somewhere else.

"Hey, Andre, are you all right?"

"Mm?" He gazed at her vaguely for a moment before his mind registered what she had said. "Oh. Yes, I'm fine. What I need right now is some serious sleep," he said, scribbling his signature onto the report, closing the file, and dropping the pen into the top pocket of his white lab coat.

"Go home. Get some rest."

"I plan to. Goodnight." He left the ER, heading for the doctors' lounge.

Twenty minutes later, Andre had changed into his riding gear and was on his way out of the hospital. He stepped through the automatic doors into the unseasonably, crisp morning air and headed for the staff car park. Once there, he straddled his motorcycle and settled into its padded leather seat. He pushed his head into his full-face, glossy black helmet and pulled on his snug, leather riding gloves, then turned the key in the ignition. He zipped out of the parking lot, merging with the traffic.

LA was a hive of activity at any hour, and as Andre whipped across the asphalt of the busy city street on his red, Ducati Monster 1100S, he couldn't wait to get home. His apartment was one of twelve in a six-story complex that had been an unused warehouse. Redevelopment had converted the building into affordable apartments, and he'd purchased his loft-style home three years after the reconstruction. It was his sanctuary.

The Emergency Room had been chaotic with no time to take a break, and he had been disappointed that Beth hadn't been rostered on the same shift. They worked well together and, from the many conversations he'd had with her, he knew they had a lot in common. His feelings for her had grown, although he tried to avoid it, and he wondered if she could possibly feel the same about him.

Riding through a quieter section of the city, Andre's mind wandered back to the first time they'd worked together, and he was recalling the moment when a black Cadillac swung out from the curb right in front of him. His mind snapped back to the present and he maneuvered around the tank-like vehicle with only inches to spare. Andre skidded to a stop across the street. How could he explain a serious accident—one he could get up and walk away from almost unscathed? He was an immortal after all, a fact that needed to remain anonymous.

The guy in the Cadillac was oblivious to what had occurred and drove away without even a backward glance. Andre watched the taillights of the Caddy disappear into the distance before starting up his motorcycle and continuing his ride home.

Andre's apartment building loomed up before him like a fortress, dark and imposing beneath the charcoal colored sky, as he rode along the familiar street. He made a right into the driveway and stopped in front of the huge gate blocking entry to the private, resident parking underneath—once the old loading dock to the warehouse. He flicked up his visor, peeled off a riding glove, pressed his thumb against the laser panel and waited for the gate to whirr into action.

The heavy, metal monster jolted off the concrete, clattering loudly as the grated steel sluggishly curled upward. Once high enough, Andre ducked his head and rode underneath. He trailed his motorcycle across the car park to his caged locker, then wandered back to the elevator, pushed the call button and waited.

When the elevator arrived, Andre pushed the gate up, stepped inside and pressed the top floor button. He stood in the center of the over-sized cubicle, reading Hemingway's 'A Moveable Feast'. Engrossed in the novel, Andre was unaware of the elevator moving past the floors and when it jolted to a stop he gazed up from the book and peered through the wooden slats. The words LEVEL SIX etched in large, white letters on the gray wall opposite peered back at him. He pocketed the paperback, shoved the gate up and stepped onto the landing. As he walked along the dimly lit corridor, his solitary footsteps echoed eerily on the marbled concrete floor of the noiseless building.

Inside his apartment, Andre shrugged out of his leather riding jacket and shoved it onto the coat rail beside the front door. He kicked off his boots and took off his leather riding pants. Underneath he wore a black T-shirt and faded blue jeans. He tossed the riding pants onto the wooden chest beneath the coat rail and walked across the moonlit living room to the panoramic window.

The glistening view of the city was awe-inspiring. He gazed at the distant city lights for a moment, then pushed a button on the wall control panel to close the massive, navy blue drapes and crossed the living room to the spiral staircase. Lack of nourishment had depleted his energy, and he climbed the dizzying stairs to his bedroom feeling lethargic.

A solitary, silver uplight standing sentinel in the corner of his room cast a soft, warm glow across the deep purple ceiling. Andre stepped onto the landing, crossed the room to his bed, undressed and immersed himself beneath the burgundy satin sheets, which felt good against his naked body. He reached for the remote lying on his nightstand and turned off the lamp.

Night enveloped him like a suffocating cocoon.

CHAPTER FIVE

Several days after the Los Feliz body discovery, Dave Colson sat in front of his computer scanning criminal MO's. It was a task he had performed more times than he cared to count since the investigation started. This time, he'd hoped to come up with anything that vaguely resembled the recent spate of murders. He stared at the files on the screen and realized it was a pointless exercise. Slumping back in his chair, he squeezed his thumb and index finger into his tired eyes and gave a heavy sigh. He'd been at it for hours.

Reece entered the workroom and spotted Dave sitting at the computer. He gave him a brief wave and then knocked on their boss's door. "Hey, Chief," he said, entering the office and closing the door behind him.

Ed Borenko had been waiting for an update. "Any new developments, Daniels?"

The detective slumped into a chair in front of the desk. "Nothing, as far as Jim could tell at the scene."

"Not a damn thing?" His boss's serious expression hardened.

Reece shook his head.

Ed swiveled around in his chair and gazed out of the window. There was a long, uncomfortable silence. He was disturbed by the news and spoke without turning back. "What's wrong with this department? Why can't we nail this bastard? Jesus, Daniels, the victims are just kids!"

"We're doing everything humanly possible. You know I'd do anything to get my hands on this guy."

Ed swung his chair back, a disturbed expression crossing his coarse features. "Then do it, Daniels! *Do* whatever it takes," he ordered, pounding a fist on the desk.

"Sure, Chief. Whatever it takes." Reece frowned at his boss. He had never seen him react this way before. The chief was a seasoned cop, who had seen pretty much everything, but the case was obviously getting to him. The detective got to his feet, crossed the room and opened the door.

"And, Daniels, keep me posted. As soon as you get *anything*, I want to know about it." He poked the air. "You got that?"

"When I get a break you'll be the first to know." He stepped out into the workroom and pulled the door shut.

Dave had been waiting outside the office. "Anything?"

"No," Reece said, irritated. "I was hoping you'd have something for me by now."

"I'm sorry, man, not one of the MO's was even remotely close to these murders." The pair headed to their desks at the end of the workroom.

"Where do we go from here? Forensics has come up with nothing so far. I don't know what else to do at this stage." Reece gave a heavy sigh. "I'm hoping the latest report will give us some kind of lead. I put a rush on it so we should have something back soon."

"What if there's nothing?"

"Then we're right where we are now. Nowhere."

As the detectives reached their desks, a young policewoman came up behind them, a stack of manila folders in her arms. "The boss said you might want to take a look at this. Just came in," she said, passing a file to Reece.

"Thanks."

She eyed them both for a moment. "Well, I'd better get back to work. See you later."

"Sure," Reece replied vaguely, his attention focused on the folder in his hand. He flung it open and scanned the pages.

"Well?" Dave asked.

"Give me a minute, will you," Reece said, his voice tight. He ran his gaze down the page. "Nothing. Dammit!" He threw the folder onto his desk, walked over to the window and leaned against the frame. Gazing at the busy street below, he said, "This bastard is laughing at us."

☙

The next afternoon, Reece made routine enquiries at local hospitals and the city's Blood Bank. None had been approached by anyone offering blood or blood bi-products. It was a last ditch effort on his part, because he couldn't get Jim's suggestion out of his head. As he drove back to the precinct, he pondered the killer's intention. What was this guy doing with the blood? And how much blood did the human body contain?

Half an hour later, Reece pulled into Hope Street outside LA's Central Library. He slapped the police permit on the windshield, covered the parking meter and approached the street-level locked entrance. The words above the doorway: *'Books Invite All: They Constrain None',* made him feel guilty for not being a frequent patron. His occupation didn't allow for much recreation time, let alone reading time, but whenever possible he enjoyed a good page turner. He climbed the stairs, entered the building and headed for the elevator.

Reece stepped out onto Lower Level Two, entered the Science, Technology & Patents Department and approached the librarian's desk for assistance.

"Can I help you?" The librarian greeted him with a smile.

"I need information about blood." Reece told her, not realizing how it sounded.

The librarian's expression changed to a questioning frown. "Blood?" she asked.

"Ah. Yes. I want to know how much blood the human body contains."

"Oh, I see." Her smile returned. "There are lots of

books you can look at; Hematology, Biology, even Human Anatomy."

"And where can I find them?" he asked, gazing at the rows of shelves around him.

The librarian glanced past him. "If you don't mind waiting a moment while I help the young man," she said, pointing past Reece, "I'll be happy to show you."

Reece glanced over his shoulder at the young couple standing behind him. He turned to the librarian and said, "I'll wait over there." He pointed to the tables and chairs nearby.

"All right. I won't be long, Mr...?"

"Detective Daniels, LAPD."

"Oh, is this police business, Detective?" the librarian quizzed.

"Unofficial police business." Reece glanced over his shoulder. The young couple had moved closer. "For my own personal reference."

The young man was more than curious. "Is it related to the murders, Detective?" he asked, stepping into Reece's line of vision.

"I'm not in a position to comment at this stage of the investigation." He didn't want to get into a discussion about the case, he needed information and that was his sole purpose for being here.

"Do you know who did it?" The young man pressed.

"I can't comment."

"The newspapers say the bodies found so far have been teenage girls. Is that true?" The young man continued. "The latest headlines are saying…"

"You shouldn't believe everything you read, son. Didn't your mother ever tell you that?" He turned to the librarian and said, "I'll wait over there until you're free. Okay?"

"Of course. I won't be long."

Reece wandered over and sat down. The morning newspaper lay folded in the center of the polished wood table. He sighed and drummed his fingers on the table top, contemplating whether to read it or ignore it. In his opinion, the headlines were never good news. He reluctantly picked it up, unfolded it and turned to the front page. "Christ!" he blurted, the sound of his voice resonating around the quiet room. He couldn't believe what he was reading.

VICTIMS OF MODERN DAY VAMPIRES

A nefarious, underground blood cult, operating in the Los Angeles vicinity, is allegedly responsible for the recent spate of teen murders. Forensic reports conclude that each victim had been completely drained of blood before the body was transported to a remote location, somewhere within the state. Police are currently investigating...

The headline smacked him in the face like an incensed lover. The department had tried to keep a lid on certain aspects of the case to prevent headlines like this, and now here it was staring right back at him. He threw the newspaper across the table. It slid onto the floor, pages scattering everywhere. Reece gazed around the room, everywhere he looked people were staring at him. Feeling enraged and embarrassed, he got up and stormed out of the library. He needed to have a word with the editor of that newspaper.

℥

"No matter what you say, Detective Daniels, explicit details to any murder investigation is big news," the newspaper editor informed Reece as he sat behind his over-sized, mahogany desk. "The readers love it. They lap it up."

"That may be, Mr. Thornton, but don't you think it's the newspaper's responsibility not to panic the public? You know how these things can escalate."

"Someone had to break the story to the citizens of this city. If we hadn't run it, someone else would have." Thornton leaned across his desk, clasping his hands in front of him. "So, Detective, what exactly are you suggesting?" The conversation had become tedious and he knew where it was going.

"I think it would be in the best interest of everyone if you print a retraction." Reece was becoming more and more irritated by the editor's self-righteous attitude, but tried to maintain a professional approach. It wasn't easy. He shifted in his seat and crossed one leg over the other.

"A retraction!" Thornton echoed. "What good would that do now?"

"A lot, I think. If people start to panic, there's no telling what could happen."

"And on who's authority … *yours*?" Thornton ignored the detective's concern. "I don't think so."

Reece was tired of getting the run around, he wanted some answers. "Who gave you the story?"

"That's privileged information. I'm not at liberty to divulge my sources." The editor enjoyed rubbing the detective the wrong way.

"Let me get this straight." Reece leaned forward. "You're telling me your *source* has proof that *vampires* exist in this city. Is that what you're saying?"

"Quite possibly," the editor replied.

Reece was fed up with Thornton's games, his cool composure cracked wide open. He grabbed the editor by the shirtfront and pulled him across the desk. "Listen, asshole, six young women are dead because of some crazy out there, and all you want to do is print lies and play pointless mind games. How can you have any leads when the department doesn't have anything solid to go on yet?" He shoved the editor back in his chair.

Thornton stood up, straightened his tie and tucked in his shirt, unfazed by the detective's sudden outburst, his arrogance intact. "What can I say?"

"You could offer to print that retraction and put everyone's minds at ease."

"Sorry, but our readers have a right to know what's going on."

"You could be charged with obstructing justice, you know," Reece bluffed.

"By printing the truth?" the editor scoffed.

"It's not the truth and you know it!"

"There are a lot of unexplained mysteries in this world. Who knows what's out there?"

"Cut the bullshit, Thornton, you don't believe that. All you're interested in is selling your goddamn newspaper. So, you won't print the retraction?"

"Not in this lifetime," the editor said, a look of satisfaction on his face.

Reece flew around the desk, fist raised ready to pop the editor right in his arrogant, pearly white smile.

"I wouldn't do that if I were you," Thornton warned. "You wouldn't want to face assault charges, would you?"

Reece wanted to put the editor in his place. He eyed him intently for a moment, then backed off. He couldn't afford to be taken off the case now, not for a lowlife like Thornton.

"If there's nothing further, Detective, I am a busy man."

"Tell me something, how do you sleep at night?" Reece strode to the door.

"I have no problems sleeping," Thornton replied, without lifting his gaze.

Reece glared at the editor. "You're a sonofabitch. You know that?"

"You're not the first person to tell me that and I'm sure you won't be the last. Close the door on your way out."

Reece flung the door open, almost ripping it from its hinges, and stormed out of the editor's office before he did something he knew he would regret later.

CHAPTER SIX

By the time he finished the Chinese take-out he'd bought on the way home it was after 8 p.m., and Reece realized he hadn't checked in with Dave. The day had been a complete waste of time he thought, remembering the incident at the library and the futile confrontation with Thornton. That sanctimonious bastard made his blood boil.

Reece dropped his chopsticks into an empty container, got up and crossed the room to the cordless phone suspended on the wall beside the refrigerator. He snatched the handset from its cradle and punched in his partner's extension. He wondered where Dave could be as he listened to the continuous ring on the other end of the line. "Pick up, Dave. Where the hell are you?" He was about to ring off when he heard a click.

"Homicide, Detective…"

"Dave?"

"I was about to call you, man. We've got another body."

"What? When?"

"About half an hour ago. Pick me up, I'll fill you in on the way."

"I'll be there in ten." He slammed the phone down and grabbed his car keys off the coffee table on his way to the front door.

⁂

Dave was waiting outside the precinct when the midnight blue Mustang screeched to a stop at the curb. Reece leaned across and threw the passenger door open. "Where are we headed?"

"Topanga State Park," Dave said, climbing in and slamming the door.

Reece pushed the blue light onto the hood and pulled out into the sea of traffic—the siren screaming. "Give me the details."

"Suspicious-looking vehicle spotted out there and someone called it in."

"Did you get a name?"

"Concerned citizen is all they said."

Reece frowned. "Of course. Anything else?"

"When the patrol car got out there, they found the girl's body in the exact location the vehicle had been seen."

"Description?"

"Black wagon, tinted windows. It would've been too far away to get the license plate."

"Okay." Reece sighed. "I want you to question the search team, see if they've come up with anything significant. I'll talk to Jim and find out what he's got so far."

As soon as they arrived at the scene, Dave made a

beeline for the uniformed guys, hoping they'd have something that could prove useful. Reece scanned the area looking for Jim, but when he got to the crime scene, he was unpleasantly surprised to see Rachel O'Grady working in Jim's place.

The pair had met a couple of years before, during a murder investigation, when she'd been called in to assist with a difficult autopsy. The moment they met there had been an instant attraction. Rachel was tall and slender with long, wavy, dark brown hair and deep green seductive eyes. Maybe what had transpired between them was purely sexual, but it had been so intense that every time they saw each other it took every ounce of their self control to keep their hands off one another. The relationship endured several months, with the passion fading long before. Now? They barely spoke, unless it was work related and absolutely necessary.

"Shit," he mouthed silently. Working with an ex-girlfriend was something he hadn't anticipated. Reece felt his gut tighten. He inhaled a deep breath and reluctantly moved closer. "Hello, Rachel. Where's Jim?"

"Not here," she replied, her back to him as she knelt beside the body.

"I can see that," Reece said, his tone curt. He was irritated by her indifference to him. "Where is he?"

"He's at home with his wife," she snapped. "Where do you think he'd be at a time like this?"

"I assumed he'd be *here* doing his job."

"You heartless bastard!" She stood up and turned her fiery gaze on him. "Are you so devoid of any emotion that you can't show some form of compassion at a time like this? What kind of man are you?" She raised a hand, motioning for his silence. "Never mind, I already know."

Reece did his best to remain civil. It was difficult. In the few short minutes they had been together she'd managed to get right underneath his skin, and not in a good way.

"Look, Rachel, let's leave our personal issues out of this … all right? We're here to do a job, and I'm obviously missing something," he said, "so why don't you fill me in?"

Rachel was about to respond, but Dave's hasty approach interrupted her. "Hey, Reece," he called.

"Give me a minute, will you, Rachel's about to…"

"No, Reece. *Now.*"

Reece turned and glared at Dave. He was irritated by Rachel's attitude, and his partner's interruption. "What is it?" he asked, walking over to him.

"There's something you should know."

"Couldn't it wait until *after* I finished talking to Rachel?" He was clearly pissed.

"No, man, this can't wait."

"Well?" Reece folded his arms across his chest. "You got me over here, so give."

"What did Rachel tell you?"

"Nothing. She didn't get a chance to."

"Good, good." Dave was relieved. He wanted to break the news.

Reece eyed him with suspicion. "Why? What's going on?"

"The murdered girl…"

"What about her?"

"She's Lisa Peters."

"And?"

"Peters … as in Jim Peters."

"Jesus Christ!" Reece paled, his breath caught in his throat. It felt as though the air had been sucked right out of him. He made his way over to the Mustang and sat on the hood.

Dave followed. "Are you ok?"

"No, I'm not ok! How could I let this happen?"

"It's not your fault, man."

"Isn't it?" He looked Dave straight in the eye. "I should've nailed this sonofabitch long before now."

CHAPTER SEVEN

'Doctor Delacroix, to emergency'. The voice over the hospital PA was insistent as Andre stepped through the automatic doors and caught the last of the announcement resonating along the corridor. He was late and had forgotten his phone. Again, the static voice nudged him into an even quicker pace.

Andre rushed along the corridor, dodging staff and patients to get to the doctors' lounge. He was about to push the door open when it swung out of his reach, and he almost ran into his friend and fellow medico, Dennis Miller.

The African-American doctor had met Andre six years before while working in the Pediatrics ward. They'd discovered they had a lot in common and had fast become friends. For the upcoming week, the pair shared the responsibility of working together in the Emergency Room.

"What kept you, man? Late night, huh?" Dennis winked at his friend as he maneuvered past him through the doorway, giving him a cheeky grin. "Hurry up. I'll cover for you."

Andre watched him stride along the corridor, through the obstacle course of waiting patients, and disappear into the ER.

Dennis wasn't sure how to diagnose the young man brought in by ambulance only minutes before. The most baffling part about his condition was the lack of wounds and the fact that he had been drained of blood to the point of death. Dennis considered the possibility the kid could be a hemophiliac, but the symptoms didn't add up. Perhaps he'd had some kind of hemorrhage, which would explain there being no wounds. Although, the paramedics who picked him up had said there had been no blood at the scene. All he could do was treat the symptoms, and wait for the pathology report. Perhaps that would give him something to go on. If not, he'd ask Andre.

Andre pushed back the curtain and stepped out of the cubicle into the sterile air of the ER. He finished filling out the patient chart at the nurses' station, handed it to the nurse sitting behind the counter, and informed her he was taking a fifteen minute break in the doctors' lounge.

As he lay on the narrow cot in the cubicle-sized

sleeping quarters, Andre closed his eyes and focused on releasing the image of blood from his mind and the counterfeit taste from his tongue. He had successfully controlled his bloodlust, and only in extreme circumstances would succumb to its demand on him. He *never* killed—only fed enough to sustain himself, which, unfortunately, was necessary. Afterward the donor would have no recollection of what had occurred, and the wounds would heal instantly, leaving no trace of the bite. He loathed being a predator. It was a legacy he definitely could have lived without.

His peaceful meditation came to an abrupt end when the door flew open and Dennis charged into the room. "There you are. I've been searching all over the damn hospital for you!"

Andre's eyes snapped open and he sat up. "What's wrong?"

"A young guy was brought in about 45 minutes ago. Almost complete exsanguination."

Andre jumped to his feet. "What do you mean?"

"Just what I said. And the most baffling part about the whole thing is there's not a single wound on his body. Not one. You want to come take a look? I could really use your input."

"Absolutely. Let's go."

Had Andre's worst fears finally manifested themselves?

CHAPTER EIGHT

The autopsy report on Jim's daughter proved just as fruitless, and as Reece scanned the pages for what seemed like the hundredth time he asked himself, "What am I *not* seeing here?"

Dave had been going over some of the other reports when he found something of interest. "Hey, I think I've got something." He came around the desk. "Look at this," he said, spreading the pages across the desk and pointing to the single printed line on each one. "This has to be a common denominator, don't you think?"

Reece examined the pages. "Why didn't we pick up on this before?"

"I don't know, man. It's been staring us in the face all along."

"Each of the victims was a virgin!" Reece slumped back in his chair. "I never thought I'd say this, but I'm stunned. With casual sex being the norm among teenagers today, there are still kids out there with some kind of moral values."

Dave wheeled his office chair around the desk and sat down. "What about Jim's daughter?"

Reece picked up Lisa Peters' file and scanned the page. "Here … yes."

"That's gotta mean something."

"Yeah. But what?"

"This guy obviously has a thing for teenage girls, and prefers them to be virgins," Dave deduced.

"Yeah, but why? He hasn't sexually assaulted any of the victims. I guess I could understand his twisted logic—wanting to be their first." Reece rifled through the papers on his desk. Something he'd read earlier popped into his head.

Dave watched him, frowning. "What are you looking for?"

"I just remembered something." He slid a computer printout from a pile of papers and scanned the page. "A lot of the kids around here frequent a new night spot called … here it is, Decadent Desire. The club has only been operating a few months, but it's succeeded in luring them away from the other popular venues around town. I think we should find out what the attraction is. Take along some photos of the victims."

"You think the club's connected to the murders?"

"That'd be too easy. But it can't hurt to take a look. Maybe someone will recognize one of the girls. At least that'll give us something to go on."

The pair gathered up the papers strewn across the

desk and stacked them into a pile. With all the research they had been doing, they'd missed the morning break. Dave was the first to realize, but only after his stomach growled its disapproval. He checked the time − 11:47. "Hey, man, you want some coffee or something?"

"Yeah. Thanks."

Dave headed to the lunch room hoping there were some donuts left.

Reece pushed his chair over to the window, sat down and gazed out at the busy street below. It felt good to stop for a while. Ever since the discovery of the first body, he'd been working non-stop. Even his social life had taken a nose dive. He didn't have a special lady in his life, one of the primary disadvantages of being a cop he knew only too well. The investigation had consumed all of his time and energy, and had fast become a personal quest to get the killer off the streets.

Thoughts of his personal life were pushed aside when he caught sight of the victims' photos and case notes scribbled on the whiteboard. He wheeled himself across to his desk, snatched up the telephone receiver and keyed in the hospital's number. He needed to talk to Andre.

"Hey, Reece, how are you doing? Sorry to keep you waiting, you know how it gets down here," Andre said.

Reece knew how it was in the ER. "Yeah, I know. I'm okay. A bit tired though." He sighed. "I think the fact that I'm not sleeping well is starting to catch up with me."

"I can prescribe something if you want."

"No, thanks. You know how I feel about induced sleep. Hey, maybe you should take some of your own advice, pal, you haven't been doing too well in the sleep department yourself, lately." They had been friends for almost ten years, but were more like surrogate brothers.

"I'm working on it."

"Can I ask you a professional question?"

"Sure."

"How much blood does the human body contain?"

"The adult body has approximately 8 to 10 pints of blood. That's roughly 7 to 8 percent of the total body weight. Is that what you're looking for?"

"Yeah, it is. Thanks. I appreciate it." He scribbled down the information.

"Anytime."

"Before I go, I've got one more question for you. How can a body be drained of blood without any wounds being…?"

"I think you'd better get down here right now."

"Why?"

"A young guy was brought in this morning. He was found in an alley down town…"

"And?"

"He was almost drained of blood, and there's no wounds on his body."

"What?" Reece jumped to his feet. "I'll be right there." He slammed the receiver down, grabbed his jacket from the back of his chair, and headed for the stairs.

CHAPTER NINE

The vampire threw back his head with a pleasurable shudder as the last mouthful of warm blood glided down his throat like exquisite, fine red wine. He released the young woman in his embrace and her lifeless body slumped to the floor. The bite marks on her skin healed instantly, leaving no evidence of his dark kiss.

He gazed at the dead flesh lying at his feet and felt no remorse. Humans were a means of survival, nothing more. He equated them to animals in a stockyard waiting to be slaughtered. They were a hollow, inferior race destined for extermination, one way or the other.

A Master vampire, he was darkly attractive with jet black, shoulder-length hair and a closely cropped goatee that enhanced his pale, striking features. Dressed entirely in black, he was a charismatic figure and exploited it to his best advantage.

It amused him that the law enforcement in the city

had absolutely no idea what they were dealing with, impossible for the collective legal mind to comprehend that the recent deaths could have been caused by *anyone* or *anything* other than a human. In his opinion, the detective leading the investigation was a pathetic fool. After a month of searching he was still no closer to the truth.

The vampire had presumed him to be far more resourceful. A misjudgment he would not repeat. That was the reason someone close to them had been chosen, and why the concerned call regarding the vehicle at Topanga State Park had been placed. He wanted to up the stakes of his game—provide elusive clues. Would the detective piece the puzzle together and believe what logic warned him not to? Would he go in search of a *vampire*? The vampire hoped he would.

CHAPTER TEN

It had been almost a week since the unnamed young man was transported to the ER. His condition had improved, although he was still on the critical list and had not yet regained consciousness. Dennis, Andre, and a small team of nursing staff worked around the clock to keep him alive. It had been touch and go for awhile, but finally his vital signs had stabilized.

Reece also kept a constant vigil on the victim's progress. He was confident that once the kid was conscious, he'd be able to fill in some of the missing pieces to the frustrating puzzle. It was obvious his attacker was the same person who had murdered the young women, and anything he could remember would bring the detective one step closer to the killer.

During that week, Reece had conducted a search of juvenile records and discovered the young man's name was Matthew Thomas. He had priors for auto theft and petty larceny. Fingerprints taken at his bedside established that. The detective also learned that the kid was nineteen, had no family living in or around LA, and was one of the countless street kids living anywhere he could find shelter.

Reece arranged for him to be placed in one of the rooms in a section of the hospital undergoing minor renovations, assuring the Director that the department would cover the expenses. After the traumatic ordeal the kid had been through, Reece wanted him to be reassured—when he regained consciousness—that he was in no immediate danger. The detective hoped Matthew could describe his attacker to a police sketch artist so that an identikit picture could be compiled.

The three men stood at Matthew's bedside.

"Any sign he'll come out of it soon?" Reece wanted answers.

"With the kind of trauma he's experienced, there's no telling how long it will take," Dennis told him.

"Well let me know the minute he does, he's our only lead. The sooner he can tell us anything, the sooner we can get this crazy sonofabitch off the streets."

"When he does, you'll be the first person we call." Andre walked Reece to the door and opened it.

"Thanks."

The pair stepped into the empty corridor. A police officer would be posted outside the room within the next half hour.

After seeing Reece out of the hospital, Andre decided to grab a mug of coffee for Dennis. As he entered the doctors' lounge, he was pleasantly surprised to see Beth having coffee with another nurse. Andre knew that any relationship was a potential risk, but hard as he tried he couldn't suppress his feelings for her.

Beth noticed him and smiled. When he reached the table her companion got up, said her goodbyes and left.

Andre sat down. "How are you? I haven't seen you in a while."

"I'm really good," she said. "I've been working in the pediatric ward."

"Oh? How do you like it?"

"The kids are great," she told him. "Some of them are so sick, but they never complain." She smiled at him. "Still working the ER?"

"Yep. I'm a glutton for punishment."

"You do a fantastic job in there. I've worked with you, remember," she said, reaching across and touching his hand.

"Thanks, but I just do what I'm paid to do."

"That's not true. You believe in what you do." Beth glanced at their hands. There was definitely chemistry between them. She caught sight of her watch. "Oh no, Sister Jacobs will be furious with me."

"Why?" Andre asked.

"I'm late, *again*," she said. "I'd better go. I'll talk to you later."

Andre watched Beth leave before getting up from the table and crossing the room to the coffee percolator. He poured a mug for Dennis and headed back upstairs.

The cop posted outside the room was reading the

sports pages of the newspaper and shoved them onto his lap when he heard the doctor's footsteps echoing along the corridor. "Hey, Doc," he said, a look of relief on his face, "that coffee sure smells good."

"Why don't you go downstairs and get yourself some?"

"I don't know." The cop checked his watch. "I haven't been here long."

"It won't take that long, and Doctor Miller and I are here."

"Thanks, Doc, I'll be right back." He folded the paper, dropped it onto his chair, and hurried along the corridor.

Andre entered the hospital room. "Here." He handed Dennis the mug. "Thought you could use this."

"Thanks. You're right about that," Dennis said, taking a cautious sip.

"How's he doing?"

"He opened his eyes. But he still seems to be unconscious. What do you make of that?"

"I don't know," Andre said. "Perhaps he is comatose."

"I thought that too at first, but…"

"What's on your mind, Den?"

Dennis frowned and shook his head. "I'm not sure." He hesitated. "It's like he's in some kind of trance or something."

Andre slid the penlight from his pocket and moved around the bed. He propped Matthew's eye open with his finger and thumb and shone the beam of light in and away. The pupil reacted. He checked the other eye. Same response. "You could be right," he said, disturbed by what the implication could mean.